Vampires

If you enjoy VAMPIRES, you'll love...

SPOOKS
MONSTERS
PIRATES
WITCHES
SCHOOL

All published in this series by Collins
Children's Books.

VAMPIRES was first published in
Great Britain in 1982 by Granada Publishing
First published in this format in 1995
by HarperCollins Publishers Ltd,
77-85 Fulham Palace Road, Hammersmith,
London, W6 8JB
1 3 5 7 9 10 8 6 4 2
Text copyright © Granada Publishing 1982
Illustrations copyright © Colin Hawkins 1982
The authors assert the moral right to be
identified as the authors of the work.
ISBN: 0 00 198168-4
This book is set in Galliard 12/16
Printed in Italy

Vampires

Colin and Jacqui Hawkins.

Collins

An Imprint of HarperCollinsPublishers

The Curse of the Vampire

Neither living nor dead, the vampire is a creature of the night. It steals through the darkness to prey on humankind, to drain them of their life's blood. And when the exhausted victims die, they in their turn become the 'undead'.

What comes out at night
and goes 'munch! munch! Ouch!'?
A vampire with a rotten tooth.

Typical 19th Century vampire lair on bleak Transylvanian hillside.

The Living Dead

You can recognise a vampire by its gaunt appearance and deathly pale complexion. Look for its full red lips, pointed canine teeth and gleaming hypnotic eyes. Notice the long sharp finger-nails and eyebrows that meet in the middle. Look for hairs in the palm of the hand and watch out for anyone who chooses to sleep in a coffin. Take care – even your best friend could be a vampire.

Where do vampire
undertakers conduct
their business?
From the box-office.

Despite its fragile appearance, the vampire is endowed with superhuman strength – a result of its diet of blood.

Vampires are not reflected in mirrors. As a result, many have been caught in barbers' shops.

Where do you find vampire snails?
On the ends of vampires' fingers.

What do vampires eat with bread and cheese?
Pickled organs!

Where do vampires keep their money?
In a blood bank.

Vampires Today

Vampires can live for hundreds of years, so long as they get plenty of rest – and blood.

What do you call a fat vampire?
Draculard!

What sort of soup do vampires like?
One with plenty of body in it.

Old vampires are especially fond of Bat-en-berg cake.

VAMPIRE'S FAVOURITE SONGS
How can I ignore the girl necks door.
Fangs for the memory.

Where does Dracula get all
his jokes from?
From his cryptwriter.

♫ Happy Birthday ♫ Dear Igor ♫ Happy Birthday
to you. ♫

Being dead and alive is not easy. Shape changing, for example – into wolves, bats, dogs, evening dress – is very wearing but often practised.

Vampire Chant
Lock your windows
Close your doors
No one is safe from
    Our fangs and claws.

Cold wet nose, glossy coat and bright eyes are signs of a happy and well nourished werewolf.

Evening Dress

Vampire bats and werewolves are easily recognisable by their dinner suits.

Cold wet nose ↓

A short whiskered, dribbling wolf in a bow tie and dinner jacket is certain to be a vampire.

Watch out for wolves, bats, dogs and men in evening dress. And listen at night for moths pinging at your window, owls hooting, cats howling. They could be the servants of a vampire – watching you.

RECOMMENDED READING LIST:-

I Saw A Vampire - by Denise R. Knockin

The Vampire's Victim - by E. Drew Blood

Dracula - by Pearce Nex.

Black Magic - by Sue Pernatural.

A Bite In The Night - by B. Warned.

Who has the most dangerous job in Transylvania?

Dracula's dentist!

Why don't vampires have balls?
Because they can't dance

Beware of owls on the prowl and moths that cough

Cough!

Cough!

15

Vampires Around the World

Bavarian Vampires

Once vampires lived only in Eastern Europe; today they live in many other parts of the world. Different nationalities have different characteristics. The Bavarian vampire, for instance, sleeps with one eye open and its thumbs linked. British vampires read The Times and carry black umbrellas. See if there is one in your street.

Bavarian Vampires are often held responsible for cattle plague.

What do you call an
old and foolish vampire?
A silly old sucker.

What do vampires do
every night at 11 o'clock?
Take a coffin break.

hat is bright
ed and dumb?
A blood clot!

"tis the work of
a Bavarian vampire
for sure!"

What kind of boat
does a vampire use?
A blood vessel.

"GASP!"

What does a vampire take for a bad cold?
Coffin drops.

What is a vampire's favourite fruit?
A neck tarine.

Transylvanian Vampires

The Transylvanian Vampire has a passion for high heels and old ladies.

Bulgarian Vampires

The Bulgarian Vampire has only one nostril.

only one nostril

What are a vampire's favourite T.V. programmes? Strange Hill and Horror Nation Street.

What do you call a vampire who gets up your nose?
Vic.

What runs in vampire families? Noses.

What is Dracula's favourite breed of dog?
A bloodhound.

Russian Vampires.

Russian Vampires are allergic to the clergy. (It is thought that the allergy takes the form of a purple face)

purple face

American Vampires.

SNORT! SLURP! SLURP!

"Mmm! What a lovely ear my dear."

What does a vampire say to the mirror?

Terror, terror on the wall!

"tis a fine night for a bite."

Paddy Von Blutto

Irish Vampires

Irish Vampires hate the taste of blood.

The American vampire's nose is adapted to suck blood from its victim's ears.

21

Vampire Lore

According to ancient texts, vampires will crumble to dust if caught in the rays of the sun. So if you wake to find a vampire leaning over you, don't panic, just try to keep it talking until dawn.

A vampire at night
is an awful sight.
And his bite
will give you
a terrible fright.

Dracula's favourite
restaurant :—
The Happy Biter.

Another remedy is to eat as much garlic as you can and breathe over the creature until it flees back to its grave.

Eeek!

Garlic breath

An old trick
to make a vampire sick...
Ruby lips with garlic spread
will save your neck
from being bled.

Mummy, Mummy, why do you
   keep poking Daddy in the ribs?

If I don't the fire will go out.

What do you call a
vampire sitting in
   the gutter?
          Dwayne.

A hole by a grave is a sure sign that it is occupied by a vampire. But neither boiling water nor smoke will disturb the sleeping tenant.

A grave matter

For centuries ordinary people have tried to rid the world of vampires, pursuing them with mirrors, garlic, sick pigs, sour milk, Christmas puddings, wooden stakes and ever more ingenious weapons. But, as fast as a new remedy is devised, it is proved useless against the supernatural cunning of the evil ones who walk by night.

The only sure way of exterminating a vampire is to drive a stake through its heart while it sleeps – not easy with the Bavarian!

You've got to be smart to stake a vampire's heart.

FOR SALE :– 1946 Mercedes Hearse
Good condition,
original body.

27

Into bed you
must tumble.
Before the dawn.
Or you will crumble.
Afore the sun
is in the sky...
Be back in bed
Or you will die!
(Vampire Nursery Rhyme)

Why did the vampire win
an art scholarship?
Because of the way he drew blood!

In America a silver bullet may be shot
through the heart, though American
vampires don't hang about for long.
A simple method of slaying a British
vampire is to steal the umbrella and
thrust it into its heart. If the vampire is
reading its paper, it will hardly notice.

Vampires at Work

Nowadays, vampires live relatively normal lives, coping with all but the brightest sunlight. Vampires are found in all walks of life.

There are vampire bus drivers, vampire lollipop ladies, vampire teachers, vampire shopkeepers, Vampire traffic wardens, vampire doctors, vampire butchers and vampire tax collectors

A Vampire Astronaut

"I'll soon have a nice hole drilled in that sir."

Dentist Vampires

"Did you know that in space no one can hear you scream?"

Vampire Doctors

I do not like thee,
Doctor Drac,
and certainly not
behind my back...
(part of an old chant.)

Favourite vampire dances :-
The Fang Tango.
The Vaults.

Be it in May, or on a
cold winter's day,
In a coffin one day,
We'll take you away.
(Traditional Undertaker's grave song)

"Open wide and I'll pop it inside"

Vampire Undertakers

The most popular choice of career of all for a vampire is to be an undertaker.

Family Life

* Note for scholars. Bluot is old high German for blood.

The Von Bluots* are a typical vampire family. They are descended from a proud and ancient family of Bavarian vampires but now live in Bradford.

Like most other British families, their day begins with a warming breakfast – a nourishing bowl of bones for all. After a quick skim through The Times, Vlad the Dad sees the children off to school and drives to his job as a civil servant.

Dracula always kept his wife awake with his coffin!

At four o'clock in the afternoon he is free to pursue his favourite sport – coffin jogging. Vlad is the local champ and is in training for the marathon.

Vlad the Dad practising for the 10,000 metres 'Race to the Grave' with full casket event.

Why was Dracula in trouble?
He was overdrawn at the blood bank.

Why is it easy to trick Dracula?

Because he's a sucker!

At Home With Mother

At home, Mum – Mrs Belladonna Plasma
Von Bluot – looks after baby Wallachia.

Her full name is Wallachia Julie Andrews Von Bluot, the family having just seen The Sound of Music for the seventh time when she was born.

A visit to the graveyard

Wallachia is nine months old, very happy, very wicked and very healthy. She has just grown her first fang.

After lunch, Mum takes the baby to visit Grandpa and Grandma.

Lunchtime

Feeding the bats in the park.

In the evening, the family take a walk in the park with their pets. Vlad the Lad has a dog called Blod and a crow called Carone. His sister Valhalla has a cat called Bloth. Bloth and Blod are constantly at each other's throats but all else is hunky-gory. Young Vlad reads horror comics to Carone; Val nurses her dolls; their parents feed the bats and talk about old times and the children's progress at school. Vlad has been bad again, sent off at rugby for biting in the scrum. But Val has come top in woodwork for making a sweet little coffin for her dolls.

Mr Von Bluot : How many people for dinner tonight?

Mrs Von Bluot : One each, as usual!

Goremet Supper

Tonight Valhalla has brought two
schoolfriends home for supper.
Despite everyone making them very
welcome, the visitors are quiet and
hardly eat a thing. They cannot even
finish their soup.

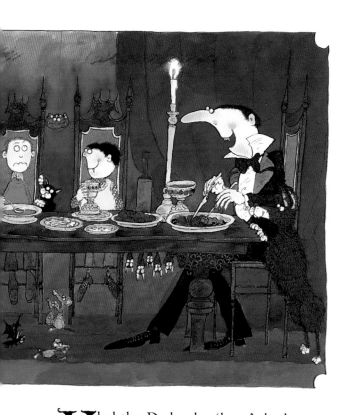

Vlad the Dad, who 'hasn't had a bite all day', sinks his teeth into the best end of neck and tries to encourage them. "Eat up, my dears, the food will make you strong and put hairs on your palms."

"Come along," says Mum, "eat up your soup. Then we'll all have some jelly belly and cream and you can go and play with your bats in the attic."

Gory Bedtime Story

Like most other children, the Von Bluots like stories about monsters and mysteries, princes and wizards, goblins and ghouls. But most of all they love to hear about their ancestors. "Tell us about Vlad the Impaler," they implore at bedtime, "and how Vlad the Glad got his fang out in time. Tell us how Vlad the Mad caught Vlad the Cad in Granny's casket. Tell us about Dracula the filmstar..."

When Dracula met his wife it was love at first bite.

We get toothache, Dracula gets fang pangs!

What is rhubarb? Bloodshot celery!

What do you get if you cross a vampire with a hot dog? A fangfurter.

Bat mobile

Vampire potty

"That's enough now, dears," says Mum. "Settle down and I'll read you a nice grim story by your uncles Jakob and Wilhelm Grimm Von Bluot."

Why do vampires drink blood? Ginger beer makes them burp!

Why are vampires crazy? Because they are bats!

"And then the monsters gobbled everyone up and lived happily ever after."

nd she reads them not just one tale but four, which only goes to show what great mums vampires make.

Look at those teeth!!

What a lovely wet nose.

Little Red Riding Fangs
Who it is said, bit on the head
a wolf in Granny's bed.

Vampire Graffiti:

VAMPIRES ARE A
PAIN IN THE
NECK!

Goldifangs and the Three Bears

The lovely story about the little girl

who loved porridge and bears' blood.

And so to bed...?

When the children are asleep, Mum and Dad watch old vampire movies on the television (there never seems to be anything else on). Afterwards they go upstairs...

11:30pm

How do you feel after you've been bitten by a vampire?
Holier!

12 Midnight

What is the scariest
fairytale of all?
Ghouldilocks and
the Brrrs!

12:02

12:02½

12·03

12·05

12·06

So remember – if a vampire flies through your window tonight, don't worry, it's only being friendly. Don't see red, it only wants to make you a vampire too. And there are far worse things to be than a vampire – and I should know.

Remember!
When they're
out at night
–vampires bite.

When the moon is full beware the hairy dog and the low flying bat.

Why don't vampires get kissed much?
Because they have bat breath!

What do polite vampires say?
Fangs very much.

When the moon is bright
We'll go out for a bite
We'll give them a fright
In the middle of
the night.

Goodnight Children
Sweet Dreams.